SERIES CANADA

JOHN IBBITSON

THE WIMP

Collier Macmillan Canada, Inc.

Series Canada Titles

Amy's Wish	Dope Deal	Ice Hawk	Spin Out
Baby Baby	Fair Play	Micro Man	Take Off
Burn Out	Fire! Fire!	No Way	The Beast
Dead On	Gang War	Runaway	The Wimp
Dirt Bike	Hot Cars	Snow Ghost	Wild One

Series Canada Teacher's Guides are also available.

Collier Macmillan Canada, Inc.
1200 Eglinton Ave. E., Don Mills, Ontario M3C 3N1

ISBN 02-947280-6

Editor: Sandra Gulland
Designer: Brant Cowie
Illustrator: Heather Collins
Cover Photograph: Paterson Photographic

2 3 4 5 6 90 89 88 87 86
Printed and bound in Canada.

CANADIAN CATALOGUING IN PUBLICATION DATA

Ibbitson, John.
  The Wimp

(Series Canada)
ISBN 0-02-947280-6

I. Title. II. Series

PS8567.B34W55 1985   C813'.54   C85-099550-7
PR9199.3.I22W55 1985

CONTENTS

CHAPTER

1

It was 8:57, and I was standing next to the water fountain near room 108. Each morning for the last six weeks I'd been standing next to the water fountain near room 108. Don't get me wrong, it's not all that great a water fountain. As fountains go, I'd say this one was just all right.

I was there because room 108 is Laura Bronstein's home room. You can count on it—if you stand by the water fountain at 8:57, you'll see Laura go in room 108. And this morning, like all the other mornings, Laura came by. And walked into room 108. And didn't see me.

I sighed, and leaned over to take a drink from the fountain. It splashed me in the eye like it always splashed me in the eye. But you get used to water fountains splashing you in the eye... when you're a wimp.

It's not that I ever *wanted* to be a wimp—it just happened. If you met me, you'd think to yourself, "This guy's a wimp." My dad thinks I'm a wimp, my pet rabbit Simpson thinks I'm a wimp, even my mother thinks I'm a wimp, though she calls it "cute."

Anyway, I'm used to it. The way I see it, anyone who's seventeen has a crisis. It doesn't matter who you are, if you're seventeen you've got a crisis. Maybe you're crazy in love with someone who thinks you make a good doormat. Maybe your grades would make you laugh if they didn't make your parents cry. Maybe.... Well, it doesn't matter, life has its problems when you're seventeen. What I don't like is that I have all those problems, and I'm a wimp as well.

I left the fountain and headed for home room. It takes me a while to get to home room, but then it takes me a while to get anywhere. For some reason I keep bumping into people. I don't want to bump into people. I have to spend so much time saying I'm sorry, and picking up my books....

Anyway, there I was, as usual, trying not to bump into anyone who looked really mean, when I heard my name.

"Randy! Hey, Randy, wait up!"

It was Gorf.

Gorf has real problems—I mean *real* problems—and one of them is he doesn't know it. Gorf doesn't know he talks too loud, or that he talks too much, or even that his duck jokes aren't funny.

And there he was, coming down the hall wearing a stupid grin and a sweater that made me think of a TV test pattern. Sometimes I think I'm Gorf's best friend because he makes even *me* look good.

Truth is, I like Gorf. I know he acts stupid and dresses stupid and makes too much noise, but I like him. He's there when you need him, and I think that's what counts most. His only real problem is he gets ideas.

Gorf gets ideas the way I get pimples —like the time he wanted to beat the odds by buying a hundred lottery tickets at once. There's not much you can do with a hundred losing lottery tickets.

Or the weekend he talked me into going to Halifax to see a rock concert that was sold out. Only Gorf knew it wasn't *really* sold out. You can always get tickets at the last minute, he said. You know something? Some rock concerts that are sold out are *really* sold out.

Well, I've been living with Gorf's ideas since I was ten and I'll admit I even like them sometimes. Life isn't boring with

Gorf around. And like it or not, I could see another idea coming.

"Hello, Gorf," I sighed.

"Hey, guy, how's it going? Listen, what happens when a duck flies into a bakery?"

Why did Gorf always ask you how you were and then not give you a chance to answer?

"I don't know, Gorf," I said in that tired voice I always seem to use when I'm around him.

"It turns into salted quackers—get it? Get it?"

And that was one of his better jokes—but Gorf wanted to do more than tell jokes.

"Randy, we gotta talk," he said, looking around as though he thought we were being spied on.

"So talk," I said, knowing that I was going to be late for class.

"Not here—" he said in a whisper you could hear from the other side of Truro, "—some place private."

"Gorf," I pointed out, "no one listens to us when we want them to. Why should anyone listen to us when we don't?"

"Randy, you've got to stop putting

yourself down all the time—kids won't vote for you."

"I wasn't putting myself down—I was putting us both down," I told him.

Then what he said hit me: "*Vote?*"

"That's what I want to talk to you about—the Student Council elections that are coming up."

"You want *me* to run for Student Council?" I asked, sure that Gorf had gone over the edge.

"Of course I don't want you to run for Student Council."

"Oh." I breathed a sigh of relief.

"I want you to run for Student Council *president*."

CHAPTER

2

President? If that was funny, how come I wasn't laughing?

"Gorf, it's one of two things. Either you're joking, in which case it's not funny, or you're serious, in which case it's still not funny."

Gorf had grabbed me by the arm and was leading me past our home room.

"I'm dead serious," he said. "Look, we all know Bryce Harcourt will run."

"Wrong—we all know Bryce Harcourt will run and *win*."

You might say Bryce Harcourt was a popular sort of guy—you might also say

Elvis was a popular sort of singer.

It wasn't just that Bryce Harcourt led the basketball team to its first win ever. It wasn't just that his grades were somewhere above 100 per cent. It wasn't just that he looked like a movie star and was so friendly he even said "Hi" to *me* sometimes. No, people would say, there was more to Bryce Harcourt than that. Maybe there was, but all the rest sure helped.

And we all knew that Bryce Harcourt was going to be Student Council president this year—that is, we all knew except Gorf.

Gorf was half pushing, half pulling me down the hall. For sure we were not headed for home room, for sure we were going to miss the bell, and for sure I was going to get into trouble.

Gorf led me into the empty gym, a place I have learned to hate.

"Tell me one thing," he said as our voices echoed back and forth. "Do you like Bryce Harcourt?"

"Of course I do. Everybody likes Bryce Harcourt."

"Tell me one more thing—do you *really* like him?"

"I just said . . . ," I began, but then I shut up to think. Of course I liked Bryce Harcourt, just like all the kids liked Bryce Harcourt, but did I *really* like him?

"No," I said, "not really."

Funny, isn't it? I mean, I like Gorf, even though he drives me crazy. He was driving me crazy right now, but I still like him. So why didn't I like Harcourt?

Well, I just wouldn't want Harcourt for a friend. Gorf had his problems—boy did he have his problems—but he was so loyal that if you were his friend he'd lie down and die if you asked him. I don't think Harcourt was loyal to anything except his two hundred sweaters.

"Maybe I don't much like Bryce Harcourt, but that doesn't mean I have to run against him."

"Oh yeah?" came two voices from behind me.

I turned, and there were Freddie and Sharon, sitting on a stack of work-out pads.

Freddie, Sharon, Gorf, and I call ourselves The Group because we hang around together. I guess we really like each other, which is a good thing, because no one else did.

Freddie's a chemistry nut and, like always, he had stains on his clothes and smelled like chlorine or worse. Nice kids call Freddie "The Prof." Kids who aren't so nice call him a name I wouldn't repeat.

Sharon is so shy most people don't even know her name. When she talks, which isn't much, you get the feeling she is trying to melt into the floor.

Anyway, they are my best friends, along with Gorf. And it was pretty clear now that this wasn't just Gorf's stupid idea. It was their stupid idea, too. This whole thing had been planned.

"He won't do it," Gorf said to them.

Freddie closed his book and Sharon took off her headphones.

"Why not?" Freddie asked.

Why not? I couldn't believe this.

"For one thing, I'll lose," I said, "and for another, I don't want to be president of anything, and for a third, I'd rather die than give a speech."

"Is that all?" Freddie asked, looking at me as if all that was pretty much nothing.

"You just gotta run against Harcourt," Gorf said. "His group already goes around like they own the school—nobody is even running against him. What kind of election is it, with only one guy running? Well, they don't own me, and I wanna show the suckers."

"Show them what?" I asked.

"That we're not afraid to run against them," Sharon said quietly.

"But I'd lose."

"Then we'd show them we're not afraid to lose," Sharon went on.

I could tell this was something Sharon had been thinking about.

"Why me?" I asked.

"Because you've got style!" Gorf burst out. "You'll blow 'em away!"

I just looked at him. Who was he trying to kid?

"Well, at least they don't hate you as much as they hate me," he said with a shrug.

The bells were ringing and I wasn't about to get into trouble for something as stupid as this.

"I'm sorry—I can't," I said, because I couldn't. "I know it's the pits the way people look down on us, but running for president won't make it better."

Freddie sighed and started for the door, and Sharon sighed and put her Walkman back on.

Gorf slung his arm around my shoulder. "Yeah, it would never work," he said, as we started out of the gym.

But then he put his mouth near my ear and whispered, "Of course, if you did run, Laura Bronstein might notice you."

I stopped dead still.

Laura Bronstein.

Like a man under a magic spell, I said the fatal words—"I'll run."

CHAPTER

3

Have you ever been so hung up on someone you can't sleep? You just lie there, thinking about her and wishing you were dead, because it's all so hopeless. So you pretend, you make up scenes where you're together and it's perfect.

I was like that over Laura Bronstein. At breakfast, on the bus, in class, all I thought about was her. It was so bad my marks were falling, and they were already in the basement. But I didn't care. Nothing like that mattered—I was so in love with Laura all I could do was stand outside her home room and wrestle with the water fountain.

I suppose I could have just gone up and talked to her, even asked her out. I could also have walked on water.

I knew I couldn't keep on like this. I was going crazy and my stomach hurt just thinking about her. I guess I was building up to do something really stupid, and it just happened that Gorf came up with the best way to do it. Gorf's good at coming up with really stupid ideas.

So I did it—I let Gorf put my name up for Student Council president. Even though I couldn't come up with one good reason why I should get the job. I mean, presidents think a lot about how they can make the school better. They have meetings to talk about big things and make big plans. Every time I thought about being in a meeting like that I got dizzy.

I had two weeks—two weeks to talk students out of voting for the person they liked and into voting for a wimp instead. There have been better odds.

It didn't matter much, of course, since I was just doing this so Laura would notice me. But it seemed to me more likely that she'd notice me if I looked like a real candidate and not an idiot. But I just couldn't think of a good reason why anyone would vote for me. Even *I* wouldn't vote for me.

After the first few days things were getting pretty bad. Sharon was making posters and getting leaflets printed up. She needed a picture of me for a poster in the main hall, but the only shot I had was my grade nine photo. I looked like I had just been told my dog was dead. But it was all I had so we hung it up.

I walked up behind some kids who were looking at it. They were talking about marking it up, but couldn't think of what could make it look worse.

Freddie handed out the leaflets in the halls. Some kids took them, maybe because they made good scrap paper. But they talked to Freddie as he stood there, so I figured he might know what kind of chance we had. When we were alone together in the chem lab, I asked him what the odds were.

"In math class they're giving ten-to-one against you."

You can guess how much this cheered me up.

Still, given a choice between Freddie and Gorf working on the campaign, I'd have to choose Freddie. At least Freddie didn't cause trouble.

What did Gorf do? Gorf ran my campaign for me. Between classes, during lunch, after classes, you'd see Gorf walking down the halls with a sandwich board that read "Randy's Dandy" on one side and "Randy's Handy" on the other. He wore a straw hat, his loudest shirt, and a plastic duck on his arm. And then he would shout, "Randy, Randy, he's our man, if he can't do it nobody will!"

There may have been someone in the school who was *maybe* thinking of voting for me. If so, I'm sure Gorf changed the kid's mind.

After one week I was a wreck, Sharon was wild, and Freddie was making paper airplanes with the leaflets. But Gorf was having the time of his life and Harcourt was heading for a landslide.

And *then*, just to make things perfect, I saw Laura with a button that read, "Harcourt's the Man for Me." All in all, the campaign was turning out to be one of Gorf's real bombs.

And *then*, just when it looked like it was all over, came The Night of the Blue Moon Diner.

CHAPTER

The Blue Moon Diner was the place where all of us hung out. The food was lousy, Shirley was the meanest waitress north of Yarmouth, and the smell was like a salt marsh on a hot day. But it was cheap and they didn't mind noisy high school kids fooling around. So everyone would meet there before a party, after school, or just whenever they felt like it.

It was Friday night. Sharon, Freddie, and I were sitting in the diner, eating greasy french fries and drinking skim milk. The juke box was playing some music so old I've heard my mom sing it.

As usual, Gorf was dropping a fortune on the Gorf game we named him after. The invaders were having a field day.

All of a sudden, who should walk in but Bryce Harcourt and some of his friends. One of them was Kurt, who ran Harcourt's campaign. But I wasn't looking at Bryce or Kurt—my eyes were fixed on Laura Bronstein, who had come in with them.

My heart did the usual end-over-end flip-flop and I was having trouble breathing. But I had to look good because Laura and Harcourt were just a table away from where we sat.

I was just getting my breathing under control when Harcourt left his group, walked over to me, and held out his hand.

"Look, Randy," he said, in a voice as smooth as his beige sweater, "I want to wish you luck on your campaign. I think it's turning out to be a great race, and whoever wins, it's an honour to run against you."

Well, really.

I shook his hand and must have said something. He slapped me on the back, wished me luck, and walked back to his

table. I decided I would vote for him.

"That duck-brain," Gorf growled as he came back to the table. "He knows everybody is watching so he pulled that stunt to get votes."

I just wanted to quit. Harcourt was a decent guy and we all knew he was going to win. Besides, Laura still hadn't noticed me and now she was sitting with the enemy! It wasn't worth it.

The diner was full and a lot of kids were making noise, but it seemed that the loudest voice in the crowd was Kurt's.

Why had a nice guy like Bryce Harcourt picked Kurt to run his campaign? I knew Kurt was one of Harcourt's best friends, but he wasn't like Harcourt at all. He was good looking, all right, but not *smooth* good looking like Harcourt. And he had a temper. Kids still talk about what he did to that defenceman last year. You didn't want to get on the wrong side of Kurt. As it turned out, we were about to.

Kurt was stacking up coffee cups, though I think he had been drinking more than coffee. Laura was looking at him like he had escaped from the zoo.

Harcourt and his buddies were trying to
make Kurt keep it down.

Then there was a crash and we all
turned to look. A chair had fallen over
when Kurt stood up, and now he was
coming over to our table.

I didn't like it. It looked like Harcourt
didn't either, because he tried to make
Kurt sit down. But nobody tells Kurt to
sit down if Kurt doesn't want to sit
down . . . and Kurt didn't want to sit.

He was standing at our table, swaying
slightly from side to side. "Bryce wished
you luck, so I thought I would too," he
said.

Everybody was watching when I said, "Thanks, Kurt," and held out my hand.

Kurt took my hand and squeezed it, hard—so hard it hurt.

How could I have fallen for such a stupid trick? I tried to wriggle free, but he only squeezed tighter.

"Let him go, duck-face," Gorf warned, but Kurt just grinned and squeezed harder.

"Let go!" Gorf said, stepping in closer.

I was turning purple and tears were coming to my eyes. Would my hand ever be the same again?

I figured that Gorf was going to do something crazy, but before he could, Sharon stepped between them and gave Kurt a solid kick in the shins.

Kurt let out a surprised howl and finally let go. I looked at my hand. Would the doctors be able to save it?

"Kurt, you make a duck look smart," Gorf said, not letting up.

Kurt's voice dropped down low, like an animal's growl, "You got some problem, Gorf?"

"Just you," Gorf replied, throwing back the challenge.

Now, in a fight between Gorf and Kurt, I'd give Gorf seven, maybe eight seconds, so I thought it was time to butt in.

"Sit down, Gorf. It's not worth the trouble."

The last thing I wanted was Gorf getting massacred.

And then Harcourt was there, putting his hand on Kurt's shoulder. Harcourt was smiling, but he looked worried when he said, "Kurt, old man, it's time to go."

But Kurt wasn't listening to Harcourt, and Gorf wasn't listening to me. They stared at each other, their fists clenched.

Not a spoon was stirring in a single coffee cup. The juke box was silent, and no one dared to break the stillness. Everything was heavy and still, like just before a storm.

CHAPTER 5

I knew there was nothing either Harcourt or I could do. But if Gorf fought Kurt, Gorf would end up in that Great High School in the Sky.

Suddenly, out of nowhere, there was Laura Bronstein. She stepped in between Gorf and Kurt—not a safe place for anybody to be—and pushed them apart.

"That's enough."

Kurt looked at us, then at Gorf, then at Laura before he finally backed down.

"Sure," he said, "let's get out of here. You said it yourself, Bryce—who wants to eat in The Blue Moon anyway when jerks like Randy and Gorf think they can come here."

Harcourt's face turned a little pink beneath his year-round tan. "Now, Kurt, you know I never said that."

With Harcourt on one arm, and Laura on the other, Kurt was slowly being edged toward the door. The storm was passing.

Freddie hadn't said or done a thing through this whole scene. He'd just been sitting there, reading his science book. Now he looked up and said, quite calmly, "Kurt, you should give your life to science. Your brain is a perfect vacuum."

I was so shocked I couldn't believe I'd heard it.

But Kurt *had* heard it, and he quickly swung around, pushed Harcourt and Laura aside, and threw himself at our table before Freddie had time to move. Freddie's chair went over, and he went with it.

Kurt fell on top of Freddie, and Sharon and I jumped on top of Kurt. Gorf was there before either of us, and I saw Laura pulling at one of Kurt's legs.

But we couldn't hold Kurt back.

"Harcourt, get your goon off—" I gasped.

Kurt had one arm around my neck. He
was doing a great job of keeping me from
breathing. Kids were standing on chairs to
get a better view. But Harcourt just stood
there, shifting his feet back and forth.

"Come on, Kurt . . . ," he said, really
taking charge.

It was mean Shirley who had to drag
Kurt off Freddie, but it was a tough fight
even for her. If Shirley hadn't told Kurt
she was calling the cops, I don't know if
we'd ever have gotten him out of there.
At last Kurt stormed out, swearing,
followed by Harcourt's friends.

Bryce Harcourt was dabbing water on a stain on his beige sweater.

"Randy, I'm really sorry about that," he said smoothly, as though nothing had happened. "But you know Kurt's temper."

Laura wheeled around at Harcourt, her eyes flashing. "How could you let that happen?" she demanded, almost as if *she* was going to start a fight.

Harcourt looked stunned, and could only say, "Well...uh...I tried...."

"That's what you call trying?"

Boy, was she beautiful when she was mad.

"If that's the type of person you are, then I quit," she said, ripping off her Harcourt button and throwing it on the floor. "And Randy, if there's anything I can do for your campaign, let me know."

My mouth moved, but no words came out.

"Maybe we can meet Monday for lunch," she went on, "in the caf."

I jerked my head up and down, like a broken puppet.

"See you Monday then," she said, and was gone. Bryce Harcourt crawled away after her with only his sweater to comfort him.

"Come on, fella, we're getting you to a doctor," Gorf said, dabbing water on Freddie's face. "You need some stitches."

Freddie must have been hurting, but he was grinning so much that he didn't seem to be.

"Freddie, are you crazy?" Sharon asked, as we pulled him to his feet. "You could have been wiped out."

"A small price to pay to help the cause," he said, and his grin got even wider.

Then I knew—Freddie *wanted* to

make Kurt go crazy. He wanted to make
Kurt and Harcourt look stupid, and his
plan had worked. I wanted to hit Freddie
myself, for pulling such a stunt, but I also
wanted to hug him.

Gorf and I helped Freddie walk to the
door, but by the time we got there, a
strange thing happened. Somebody
started to clap. When we turned around,
all the kids were standing up, cheering
for us.

"Way to go!" came a shout.

And then—"*All right!*"

CHAPTER 6

When I got to school Monday, something was different—kids looked at me, but not in the same way. Word was getting around on what Kurt had done, and what Bryce Harcourt hadn't done. Kids were talking about The Group and me as heroes.

Thing was, I didn't even care—all I could think of was Laura. Laura was going to have lunch with me! I was going to have lunch with Laura! Every time I thought of it, I could hear music playing.

I got to the caf a bit early—well, about an hour early, if you want to know the truth. She wasn't there, so I sat down and

stared at my lunch. Tuna. It was always
tuna. Couldn't my mother have guessed
that today was special, that today was no
tuna lunch day? Today it should have
been roast beef.

It didn't matter—I couldn't eat much
anyway. I sat there, counting the chips on
my chocolate chip cookie, and then she
was there, sitting across from me.

"Hi," she said.

"Hi," I said back.

How could we ever hope to keep up
such a high level of talk?

"How's Freddie?" she asked.

47

"Oh, a few stitches, and some bruises, but he'll live. Gorf's got him on crutches, for effect."

She laughed, but then told me, "Kurt belongs in a cage. I'll never forgive him for doing that, and Harcourt was a fool for not stopping him."

"I thought they were your friends."

"They were never my friends!" she said angrily and grabbed her sandwich. "I don't have any friends," she added, biting into her salami and rye.

"But I always see you with people...."

"Being with people is not the same as having friends—friends you trust."

That was true.

"You can trust me," I said simply, since trust was about the only thing I had to offer.

"Yes," she said, looking at me. "I think I can. I saw that in the diner."

I think I'll die now—I think I'll just lie down and die.

Laura was looking at me.

I was looking at her.

Neither of us was looking at lunch.

It was a special moment, one to treasure for a lifetime.

Of course, that was when Gorf had to arrive.

"Hey, hey, hey—if it isn't Beauty and the Beast," he boomed.

I think I could have killed him.

Gorf clapped us both on the back, pulled up a chair, and went on, "Whadda you guys eating? I got a Cheez Whiz and banana sandwich—I just *love* Cheez Whiz and banana."

Do I torture him first, or just clobber him?

"I'm glad you joined us, Gorf," Laura said, as if she didn't mind him at all. "I want to talk about the campaign. It looks like you could use a little help."

I think Gorf was about to tell her we were doing just fine on our own, but Laura cut him off. Which was good, since I was ready to stuff his sandwich down his throat.

"You need to organize and get this campaign moving," she said.

"Whaddya call this?" Gorf replied, pointing at his signs.

Luckily, she didn't answer him.

"You need to talk to students, one-to-one," she said to me.

"Thanks, but then I'd lose for sure," I said.

"You don't have much confidence in yourself, do you?" she said, looking at me strangely.

"None at all," I replied.

"Well, at least you're not vain," Laura said, laughing.

She looked at Gorf, who was licking the Cheez Whiz off his bread. "Don't you see—you've got to make the students *see* why Randy's the better choice."

"Why am I the better choice?" I asked.

"You don't know?" she asked.

"No."

"Then why did you run?" she asked.

Now what could I tell her—that I just wanted her to notice me? I didn't have the nerve to say it.

Then I remembered what Gorf had said at the very beginning. "I don't think kids want Harcourt's group to go around like they own the whole school," I said. "So I'm giving them a choice."

Gorf choked on his Cheez Whiz, but Laura was impressed.

"I think you'll make a very good president," she said, and I could tell she meant it.

"Now, about the campaign . . . ," she went on.

She talked about how we should split up the student body into groups with each of us working on one group. She talked about how many new voters we had now, and how to organize them. It was clear from what Laura said that she'd been doing a lot of thinking.

Gorf was munching on his sandwich, but I could tell he wasn't happy. I knew what he was thinking—that he was getting shut out of things—and that wasn't fair.

"Laura," I said, "this is great, but, well, Gorf's my manager, and . . . well, I sort of do what he says."

Laura was surprised and for a moment she didn't say a word. Then she started to collect her lunch. "Of course, it was rude of me. I didn't mean to butt in . . . ," she said, starting to get up.

I wanted to cry—it was over between us, and it hadn't even begun. We hadn't even made it to dessert.

But Gorf was on his feet. "Randy, you nerd, there is no campaign manager. You and Laura take care of all that stuff and let me get back to my beat!"

He turned to me quickly and whispered, "Thanks, guy."

Then he grabbed his sandwich board, his hat, and his duck.

"Did you hear the one about the duck that went to jail? For safe-quacking—get it? Get it?" he laughed. And off he went, heading out to the hall. "Randy, Randy, he's our man. If he can't do it, nobody will!"

Laura blushed and turned to me, "I guess I didn't handle that very well."

"That's O.K.," I said. "It's just that a

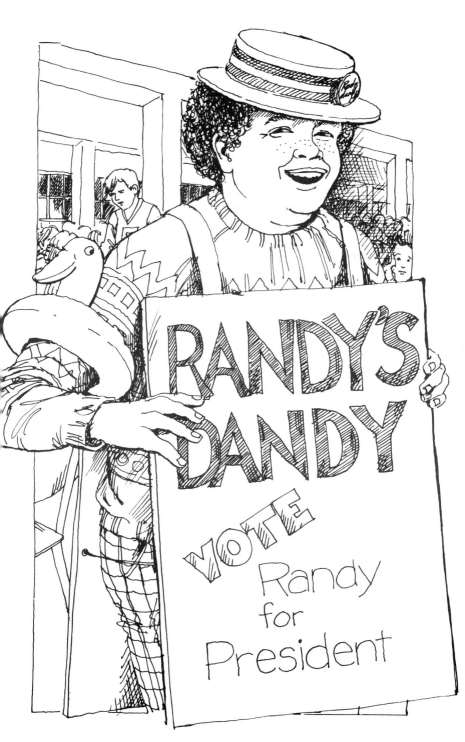

lot of people take Gorf for granted, so I
try not to."

"I think that's why I like your group,"
Laura said, giving me a smile that got
my pulse racing.

She talked more about the campaign,
but I wasn't listening. I was thinking
about her ... and me ... how things had
changed. Last Friday everything seemed
hopeless, and now—what if I won?

CHAPTER

7

After that things got pretty wild. We found that we were getting kids to support us, and the mix was really surprising. Like Tracy Holmes, the school's favourite cheerleader, who gave us her support and her pompoms. We teamed her up with Larry Parkes, who stutters but who really wanted to help. We got them both making up more posters and handing out flyers.

Laura organized us all. She gave us lists of names, and told us to talk to the kids and find out what they wanted. She said we should let students know that we were prepared to listen.

Gorf carried on carrying on and the funny thing was, it was starting to work. Kids were getting used to him, so they smiled and cheered as he walked by in his sandwich board. Gorf had become our mascot.

Even Freddie got back to work. He walked around on his crutches, handing out leaflets and showing his bandages. I think he liked getting out of the chem lab for once.

Sharon still had a hard time handing out buttons and flyers. Sharon is so shy she gets nervous standing in a movie line,

but she tried hard and helped Laura a lot by drawing up lists of names.

The only one who was useless was me. People were thinking of me now as the brave little guy who was taking on the big show-off. But each time I opened my mouth, I knew they remembered the real me—Randy the Wimp.

So Laura told me to walk around, but not to talk much. I was supposed to look like I was Thinking Important Thoughts.

Bryce Harcourt and Kurt weren't sitting still, though. They had lots of students on their side before, and they

had lots of students on their side now.

But we had one big thing going for us —no one thought we could win. We were the "underdogs." And anyone who's run a race can tell you it's easier to go after the leader than to be the leader.

But Harcourt had one even bigger thing going for him—he could give a speech without throwing up. I think he even *liked* giving speeches. When I thought of giving a speech I got the whirlies.

Laura and I worked on my speech each day after school—or maybe I should say she worked on the speech and I sharpened her pencils.

Finally, the day before the assembly, I tried the speech out on The Group. Gorf looked at Sharon, Sharon looked at Freddie, and Freddie looked at a spider crossing the floor.

"He'll sound better when he's up on stage," said Laura.

"Sure," muttered Freddie, "there's nothing like staring at hundreds of people to calm the nerves."

Thursday was the day of the speeches and Thursday morning I woke up sweating. It got worse at breakfast, and

by the time I got to school I looked like a
wax dummy in a rain storm.

"Randy! What's the matter?" Laura
asked when she found me. "You're all wet!"

"The sp . . . the . . . the . . . speech," I
blurted out. "I can't do the speech."

Laura grabbed me by the shoulders—
"Listen to me—all I want is for you to do
your best. *Don't blow it.*"

And she walked away.

In my worst nightmare, things weren't
this bad. I had never really wanted to
win. I only wanted Laura to notice me.
Well, she had noticed me and she was

doing everything she could for me. And I was going to let her down—I couldn't give that speech.

I went through classes in a daze. I was almost sick in French, though I always feel sick in French. Between classes I felt worse. Kids would grin and give me a thumbs-up sign, clap me on the back, and say, "Go for it, Randy."

Go for it? I didn't even know where *it* was.

When the bell rang for the assembly, I had made up my mind. All the students headed for the gym, and I headed for my locker. I could only think of two things—I couldn't give that speech and Laura would never forgive me.

As I walked down the empty hall I could hear noises from the gym, so I sneaked a look inside. If ever there was any doubt, that ended it—hundreds and hundreds of bodies, all sitting there, waiting for the speeches. Waiting for me.

At that moment I felt a hot breath on my neck. I jumped, but a hand grabbed my shoulder.

"Hello, Randy."

It was Kurt.

"Taking a look at the crowd, Randy?"

I was silent.

"Know what kind of speech you're going to make?" he asked, though his voice told me he already had an answer. "A wimp speech—you're going to make the wimpiest speech of your life."

Kurt's grip on my shoulder tightened and my eyes started to water.

"I don't want Bryce to lose, Randy," he said, almost gently, but I knew he wasn't thinking gentle thoughts. "In fact, I especially don't want him to lose to jerks like you and your dumb group."

The Group. I could see them through the half-open door, looking around, wondering where I was. They had all taken chances, had pushed themselves hard—and all for me. Now what was I doing for them?

"All right, Randy, you know what to do," Kurt said. He slapped my back and walked away, whistling.

And I did know what to do—I opened the door and headed for the stage. Nobody could force me to let The Group down. Even if I just stood and read from the telephone book, I was going to give a speech.

CHAPTER

8

By the time I got backstage all the others
were set to go on. Mrs. Sampson, the
principal, was trying to get the kids quiet.

"Now—those running for Council get
five minutes each to speak and the two
running for president get ten. The order
will be Bryce Harcourt and then . . . ."
Mrs. Sampson looked at me.

"Sorry, son, I forgot your name."

Things were not going well.

When we walked on stage there was a
lot of clapping. There was also a lot of
hooting and jeering, and I wondered if the
jeers were for me.

Harcourt acted like I wasn't there, while Kurt stared at me from the front row, like a bulldog in a dark alley with a kitten. I looked like the kitten.

The students running for Council stood up one by one and made their speeches. I didn't hear them thanks to the roaring in my head, like a crowd yelling at a boxing match.

Laura was sitting with The Group, watching me, leaning forward. Freddie was sitting in a wheelchair—which I thought was a bit much—talking to Gorf, who was grinning and waving his duck.

Sharon was staring at me, biting her lip as if she was the one about to give the speech.

"And now for the speeches for Student Council president. . . ."

It was time. Luckily, I didn't have to go on yet. I don't think I could have gotten out of the chair.

It was Harcourt's turn first. I thought Mrs. Sampson was going a bit far when she called him "the great Bryce Harcourt." But maybe Harcourt was that great—all the clapping seemed to show it.

Harcourt started out telling us about his favourite trophies, "the ones I'm really fond of." Then he told us about when he was young, and all the wonderful things his father had once told him. Finally he told us what he would do if he became president.

"I think it's time for a new beginning for this school," he said. "It's time we reached out and took the chances that are waiting for us. It's time for us to start building a great new future—a future of hope, a future of light and truth and . . . ."

Yeah, but what did any of this have to do with getting more dances? I thought.

"There may be some who doubt that we can be great...."

Who? I wondered.

"There may be some who want us to go backward, to give up. But I say to you," and he pointed, "and you, and you—"

Oh, brother!

"—that this is not a time to go backward, but a time to go forward, a time to reach for the stars. With your help and trust, I will work to make that dream come true. Together, there is nothing we cannot do."

He bowed his head and said, "Thank you."

I almost choked.

Then Mrs. Sampson stood up.

It was my turn! *I had to say something.*

Mrs. Sampson began, "It's now my pleasure to call our last speaker, the second student running for president... uh...."

She'd forgotten my name again!

"The...uh...the other candidate!" Mrs. Sampson said, always quick on her feet.

That was my cue to stand up—so I stood up. So far so good.

Moving was harder, but somehow I
moved and soon found myself in front of
the crowd. I looked out at the hundreds of
faces, all waiting for me to speak.

I opened my mouth. Nothing came
out. I tried again. Nothing.

Kids were moving around in their
chairs. Panic was rising up through my
chest, choking my throat as the kids
started laughing and whispering.

I turned around and looked at Mrs.
Sampson, hoping she'd come up and get
me out of this. But there she sat, looking
as if she wanted to say, "Now you know

why I can never remember his name."

And there sat Bryce Harcourt, smiling softly, thinking about what he would do after he was elected.

And there sat Kurt, right up front. He looked as happy as a bulldog that had just beaten up a kitten. When he saw me looking at him, he even waved.

He shouldn't have waved—even I have limits. I *had* to say something, so I tried to get out a sound. I used every muscle I had—both of them. "The...." It came out like a shriek. I heard someone giggle. Never mind. *Try again.*

"The ... the first thing I will do . . . ."

Something came out! There was shushing and people looked up.

What was I going to say? I couldn't remember a word of Laura's speech. Then it hit me—there was one thing I really wanted to say, no matter what happened, so I might as well say it.

"The first thing I will do as president of the Student Council . . . ."

Should I? Why not?

"The first thing I will do is introduce myself to Mrs. Sampson."

There was quiet for a moment as they figured it out, and then a big laugh. I turned and smiled at Mrs. Sampson, who did not smile back.

"The second thing I will do . . . ."

What second thing? There was no second thing—until, suddenly, the second thing popped into my head.

"The second thing I will do is ban all T-shirts with an animal sewn on the pocket."

Bryce Harcourt was, as always, dressed in a designer T-shirt worth more than my dad's best suit. The students were laughing again.

A third thing?

No, don't try it again!

"To tell you the truth, there's not much I'll do for you as president," I went on.

Well, there wasn't, so why not admit it?

"All I can promise is that I'll try to find out what you want, and I'll try to do it if I can. And I'll try to run the Student Council as well as I know how."

Did I see heads nodding along with me? After all, what more could they ask from a president?

I looked at Laura as I got ready to finish off. Her hands were tight with excitement as she stared back at me. And then I looked at Gorf, and Freddie, and Sharon, all sitting there. The Group. No one thought we were worth much, but we'd come a long way. For all of them, it was time to give the speech one last shot.

"And one more thing," I said. "Above all else, I promise that if you elect me, I will never, ever, go around acting like *I* was doing *you* a favour."

And I sat down.

Everyone clapped. A lot of people cheered. A few stamped their feet.

I'd done it.

CHAPTER 9

I was sort of mobbed by Laura and The Group when I left the gym.

Freddie made the world's quickest recovery and jumped out of his wheelchair.

"It was a great speech," Sharon smiled softly, "and I'm proud of you."

"Decent! Really decent!" Gorf yelled, letting out war whoops and blowing on his duck call like crazy. "I *told* you you were perfect!"

"What did you think, Laura?" I asked, between Gorf's shrieks and quacks. "Did I do good?"

"You did good," she said, squeezing my arm and flashing the smile that curled by toenails.

The students would vote the next day and there was nothing we could do but wait. I decided to walk home from school alone because I needed a little time to think. My life had changed so much in only two weeks. Who'd have guessed that the election would have ended up a close race?

I turned down the alley that is a shortcut to my house and broke into a jog I was so happy. I knew I might not win, but I was sure giving Harcourt a good run. And Kurt wouldn't be any too happy, right now.

Just as I was thinking that, there was Kurt. And here I was—alone with Kurt, in an alley.

"That was a pretty good speech," he said in a quiet voice.

"Thank you," I replied, though I had a hunch he wanted to do more than pat me on the back.

"Maybe good enough to win."

"Well," I said, "we won't really know until tomorrow."

"No," he said, "we're *never* going to know . . . because you're going to drop out of the race."

"What?"

"You've got until five o'clock to withdraw your name. It's 4:10 now, so if you're quick you can still make it."

"No." I said, flatly. This was probably going to hurt, but I wasn't backing down.

Suddenly Kurt became sweet and smiling. "So what can I do for you, Randy? What do you need? Money? Clothes?"

"Are you trying to bribe me?" I asked, not sure I could believe this.

Kurt stepped forward. There was fear in his voice. "Look, Randy, this can't mean all that much to you. You were just running as a joke. What if you win? You'd make both Bryce and me look like jerks. Bryce already blames me for creaming Freddie and he'll never let me live it down if you win."

"My friends are counting on me, too," I said, trying to sound cool.

"Look, I'm not *asking* you, I'm *telling* you," he said in that voice I had heard before. This was where it could get nasty.

"I'm tired of you, Randy," he went on. "I'm tired of you and your creepy friends. I tried to talk you out of it, but that's how you want it. This is your last chance to save your face, so let's start walking back to the school."

"Over my dead body."

Did I say that?

Surely I didn't say that.

As it turned out, I didn't say that—Bryce Harcourt said it. He'd been watching us from the entrance to the alley.

"Clear out, Bryce, I'll handle this myself," growled Kurt, but I could see even he was surprised.

"Not this time, Kurt," Bryce Harcourt said firmly. "I asked you to run my campaign because I thought you would handle the job like a decent guy, but I see I was wrong."

This wasn't the Harcourt I knew and disliked.

"You can't tell me what to do," Kurt said, rubbing one fist into the other palm.

"Yes, I can. I can always tell people like you what to do."

Kurt and Harcourt stared at each other for what seemed like forever, then Kurt swore, and stormed past me.

"I let you down once, in the diner," Harcourt said to me, "and I didn't want to let you down this time." He stuck out his hand and added, "May the best man win."

I guess sometimes a guy can surprise you. Harcourt may be good looking, smart, and popular—but if you give him a chance he's O.K. Deep down inside, Harcourt is a guy you could learn to like —I mean *really* like.

The next day, classes ended early and we lined up at the ballot boxes to vote. The Group sat in a classroom, drinking pop and waiting. Bryce Harcourt and his bunch were in the caf. It had been almost two hours since the vote, and still there was no word.

I kept hoping to see Laura walk through the door. First of all it's always nice to see Laura walk through the door, and second, she was checking the count. She would be the first to know who had won.

No one said much. Freddie tried to read a book, but it must have been a hard one, because he hadn't turned a page in over an hour. Sharon had her Walkman on, listening to music. She always said when life got to be too much, The Who

was the only answer. Only Gorf was acting normal, if that's what you would call it.

"Know why ducks have flat feet?" he asked. We had heard this joke before. "To stamp out forest fires. Know why elephants have flat feet? To stamp out burning ducks—get it? Get it?"

No one even blinked, so he sat down and was quiet, which must have been the first time.

There was only one thing I was thinking—*who won?* Ever since the speech, I had felt different—I *wanted* to be president. I had a few ideas about how things should be run, to tell you the truth. I should have thanked my lucky stars just to be this close, but now—now I wanted to *win*. It wasn't that I had stopped being a wimp—I'll always be a wimp—but I wanted to be a wimp who comes out on top.

It was so tense, I felt like going outside just to scream for a few minutes to make me feel better. Then Laura walked into the room.

She looked at me and I looked at her. I could tell from the look on her face who

had won . . . and I felt the bottom fall out of my stomach.

Gorf hit his fist on a table and turned away. Freddie looked out the window and Sharon put her arm around my shoulder.

It was strange, though, because I didn't feel so bad. We had all changed, thanks to the election. We all felt different about ourselves, now. And we knew, like we'd never known before, how much we mattered to each other.

There was one thing I had to know, though. "Was it close?"

Laura looked away for a second and whispered, "No."

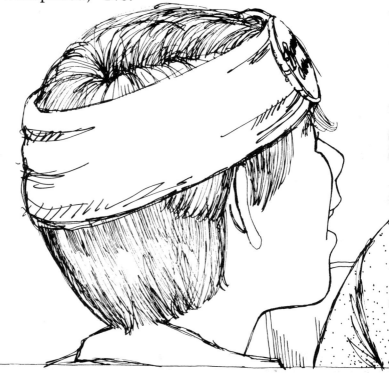

And then she turned and started laughing—"You won by a landslide!"

CHAPTER 10

So there it is, folks. Randy the Wimp is Student Council president. I'm president at school through the week, *and* at night, *and* on weekends, *and* any time some kid's got a beef. I'm the guy to call when anyone is unhappy with the way the pop machine works. It's a great job—if you want to give up any life of your own.

The kids at school still think I'm a wimp, but they kind of like having a wimp for president. After all, if I can be president, *anyone* can.

My dad doesn't call me a wimp any more, though my mother still says I'm "cute." They gave me a designer T-shirt for my birthday—one with an animal on it. What could I say?

Bryce Harcourt was a good loser. He even asked to become my "Special Assistant," which means he comes up with all sorts of ideas that I should make happen. He's sort of a high class Gorf, if you know what I mean.

Laura and I go out a lot, now. She takes me to movies, she takes me to parties, she even asked me to the Spring

Prom. I think we're in love—at least, I know we're very busy.

All in all, I have ten times the work, ten times the worry, and twice the pimples I used to have.

But I can handle all that. In fact, just between us, I'm having the time of my life.

There's only one problem and it worries me. In fact, it has me scared to death. It's Gorf. . . . You see, he just called. He's on his way over. He has another idea.

About the Author

John Ibbitson was born in Gravenhurst, Ontario, where he wrote his first play for the high school drama club. His second play, *Catalyst*, also for the drama club, was published, and is still being performed in high schools. Since then he has written numerous works. *Mayonnaise*, a comedy in two acts, was also published, and adapted for television by the C.B.C. *Mayonnaise* and *Country Matters*, another comedy, were staged by the Phoenix Theatre of Toronto. As well, he has written articles and plays for various newspapers, magazines, and theatre companies, including *The Globe and Mail*, *Performing Arts in Canada*, and The Muskoka Festival. John Ibbitson now lives and writes in Toronto.

If you enjoyed this book,
you might also enjoy reading...

BURN OUT
Bob and Chewie have a plan to catch the firebugs on
Maple Street. The plan seems good at first. But when it
backfires, they get trapped in the basement of a burning
house.

DEAD ON
What is making the strange noises in the hall outside
Larry's room? It can't be a ghost. Larry doesn't believe in
ghosts. But someone—or something—keeps leading him to
the attic of the old house.

FIRE! FIRE!
Deea joined the crew to fight forest fires. She didn't
expect to have to fight her boss, too. She knew it was
dangerous to follow Good Boy's orders. And now she is
trapped in a blazing fire—with him.

RUNAWAY
Kathy wishes she were a goldfish. She has some good
reasons—her father gets drunk and beats her, her best
friend drives her crazy, and her boyfriend wants to get too
friendly. Will she be better off if she runs away?

WILD ONE
Kate saves Wild One from Banner's whip and gets to train
the horse herself. But that's only a start. Can she prove he
can race before it's too late?

How many books in **Series Canada**
have you read?

AMY'S WISH
BABY, BABY
BURN OUT
DEAD ON
DIRT BIKE
DOPE DEAL
FAIR PLAY
FIRE! FIRE!
GANG WAR
HOT CARS
ICE HAWK
MICRO MAN
NO WAY
RUNAWAY
SNOW GHOST
SPIN OUT
TAKE OFF
THE BEAST
THE WIMP
WILD ONE

For more from the authors of **Series Canada**,
look for **Series 2000.**